THE EDUCATION OF CHILDHOOD

MAXWELL PRESS

THE EDUCATION OF CHILDHOOD

EDWARD LEVOISIER BLACKSHEAR, A.M., L.L.D

Principal Prairie View State Normal and Industrial
College Prairie View, Waller County, Texas
Active Member National Educational Association
and
Fellow American Associtaion for Advancement of
Science

MAXWELL PRESS

Chennai   Trichy   New Delhi

MAXWELL PRESS

This edition has been published in india by arrangement with Carson Books, UK

ISBN 978-93-90877-28-7   Maxwell Press

All rights reserved   No. 44, Nallathambi Street,
Printed and bound in India   Triplicane, Chennai 600 005

MJP 1053   © Publishers, 2023

Publisher : C. Janarthanan

Publisher's Note

The legacy of a country is in its varied cultural heritage, historical literature, developments in the field of economy and science. The top nations in the world are competing in the field of science, economy and literature. This vast legacy has to be conserved and documented so that it can be bestowed to the future generation. The knowledge of this legacy is slowly getting perished in the present generation due to lack of documentation.

Keeping this in mind, the concern with retrospective acquiring of rare books has been accented recently by the burgeoning reprint industry. Maxwell Press is gratified to retrieve the rare collections with a view to bring back those books that were landmarks in their time.

In this effort, a series of rare books would be republished under the banner, "Maxwell Press". The books in the reprint series have been carefully selected for their contemporary usefulness as well as their historical importance within the intellectual. We reconstruct the book with slight enhancements made for better presentation, without affecting the contents of the original edition.

Most of the works selected for republishing covers a huge range of subjects, from history to anthropology. We believe this reprint edition will be a service to the numerous researchers and practitioners active in this fascinating field. We allow readers to experience the wonder of peering into a scholarly work of the highest order and seminal significance.

Maxwell Press

The Education of Childhood.

THAT part of the period of adolescence which lies between the ages of five or six, and thirteen or fourteen years of age, and which we shall call "childhood" for the purposes of this article, is the period of greatest natural nerve response to sensor stimuli from environment, of greatest motor response to sensor re-actions, and of the greatest cerebral plasticity—the period in which mind-growth is most certain and vigorous. It is the period in which the mind is forming and is most active. It is the period in which perception or ideation is most intense and its results most permanent. The sense-percepts, the motor-impulses, formed in this period, lie at the basis of all subsequent mental life and development. This period we may call childhood, and the child is, in an important sense, more intellectual than the man, except along the lines in which man has had special training and experience.

In manhood the active powers, in both their physical (or physiological) and psychological aspects, predominate, from the necessity of the life struggle. In the child, mind, as imagination and curiosity, is dominant. There is the desire to know, to ascertain, for the sake of knowledge and the satisfaction of know ing. Childhood is the period when knowledge, fun damental knowledge, is most efficiently attained When the mind is matured it is busy, not in the acquisition of new ideas, but in the organization of experience and action about the fundamental ideas acquired in childhood. The fundamental sense-per cepts of childhood may be considered as centers about which subsequent mental experience is grouped. Hence the importance of primary edu cation, as it really and powerfully influences the organization of the content of all after mental experi ences, while the vividness or vigor of the perceptive action of the mind in childhood determines the tone or intensity of the mental life of the adult.

An error in educational practice, one that violates the law of efficiency, is that of a horizontal division or arrangement of subjects or studies as primary grammar-school, and high-school subjects, respect ively. Whereas all the broadly differentiated sub jects of educational value possess phases correspond ing respectively to the phases of the educational development of adolescence, broadly indicated by the grades of school life and the threefold grouping of the grades or yearly curricula, into primary, gram mar, and high-school groups. And the varying aspects or phases of subjects of educational study and practice correspond to the age and development of the child, while methods of instruction must correspond on the one hand to the development of the child, and on the other to the corresponding development of the subject. That is, the arrangement or development of studies should be vertical, each of the essential branches of study beginning in the lowest grade in elementary form.

Take, for example, the subject of physics, which in some curricula is not undertaken until the high-school period. It is evident that there are phases of this subject (the educational as well as practical value of which is coming into growing appreciation) which are fully within the scope of the interest and intelligence of the child, even of the lowest, or first primary grade.

A natural beginning would be with the properties of matter, those which are discovered by sense-perception, excluding such a property as impenetrability, which is apprehended philosophically or logically. The phenomenal or perceptive aspect of physics is what can and should be presented to the child of the primary school. Such properties as hard, soft, rough, smooth, velvety, elastic, heavy, light, brittle, sticky, oily, are comprehensible to little children and can be illustrated by actual objects or substances, presented in the class-room. The three states of matter can easily be illustrated by a piece of ice on a hot stove or other hot surface. The child will see the ice become water and he will see the vapor accompanying the steam. Simple physical experiments are quite in order in the primary grades. Small children take note of physical phenomena. They are interested in the ignition and burning of a match, in the flight of a toy balloon. In the class-room, experiments in capillary attraction, in electrical and magnetic repulsion and attraction, simple experiments, of course, to illustrate the more obvious and more simple effects of natural forces, could profitably be performed by the children, under direction. During the four years of the primary school, a graded course of observation and experiment is possible, that would aid in developing the perceptive powers and in acquiring fundamental ideas to be organized later as real science, or knowledge causally connected and logically arranged. The aim here would be to lead the child to see that behind phenomena are forces of nature explaining them—that there is law, order, system, in nature, despite her contrary appearance—and to identify and classify these forces.

It is erroneous, the belief that the normal child of five or six years of age has no idea of cause or force in the physical world. Of course he gets it unconsciously from his experience at home, from the expressed opinions and conduct of his parents and older members of the family. Simple as this conception is to us, that of cause, physical, explainable cause and order in nature, it marks one of the greatest distinctions between the Oriental mind and civilization and the Western mind and civilization. The vast hordes of Asia, despite a certain art culture and depth of philosophy, yet live in an atmosphere of intellectual and moral darkness because they are devoid of the idea of law and order in the physical world which every American child of seven or eight possesses. Hence, the Asiatic lives in a world of superstition, peopled with forms and forces of gloom, horror and terror.

In no respect is the white man's superiority more patent than in his conception of nature as an orderly system proceeding uniformly. And on this he bases his science, his machinery, and his inventions and discoveries. He has a foot-hold, intellectually; a standpoint; a starting place. But the Oriental mind is lost in the trackless wastes and bottomless quagmires of superstition and unchecked, unordered, metaphysical speculation. And the highest achievement of the Oriental is the development, not of the mind proper, but of certain abnormal physical powers of the brain, as manifested in alleged "psychical" phenomena—phenomena which in reality are not psychic, that is, not really psychological or mental, but actually physiological—appertaining as they do to the brain, which is a material or physical organ, and not to the mind, which is immaterial and unphysical. We say the mind is immaterial because its basic phenomenon consciousness is not apprehended or apprehensible by the senses, and all mental phenomena may be considered as developments of consciousness.

The child of five or six years of age has an idea of cause, of force in the physical world about, and such a child frequently asks questions which indicate clearly that he is interested in the causes of physical happenings. The writer recalls vividly the questions of a little boy, a relative of the family for whom he (the writer) was working in a garden. This happened over thirty years ago, while the writer was making his way through college. This little boy would ask interesting questions. One day, after a shower, he wanted to know where the rain came from. When told that the rain came from the clouds, he wanted to know what the clouds were and where they came from. When told of the great ocean from which the clouds arise, he wanted to know who made the great ocean water. When told God made the ocean, the boy asked, "Who made God?" This child was not flippant, he was serious. And yet there was nothing precocious about him. He was just a normal child. And every child has this inquisitive spirit, this undeveloped, philosophic instinct.

THE EDUCATION OF CHILDHOOD.

Every normal child is both a scientist and a philosopher in embryo. He thirsts to know facts and even more so, to know the why of these facts. But present methods of child-rearing tend only to suppress the child's spirit of inquiry and to stamp out the spirit of initiative and spontaneity. These methods are methods of manufacture rather than of true culture of the child's powers. Their effect is to produce a Chinese-like uniformity and sameness rather than to develop the individuality and personality of the child. Intellectuality in a child is regarded as an abnormal symptom, and it seems to be believed that the wise child, like the good child, will die young—unless his desire for wisdom is checked. It was this superstition that led a certain parent, who was alarmed by his child's questionings about the origin and meaning of certain familiar phenomena, to give the child a course of laxative medicine. His child craved intellectual food, but was given pills. In later educational life, the boy who possesses an unusual craving for knowledge— a passion for studies—is ridiculed as a "grind." The effects of this widespread universal suppression of the manifestation of positive vigorous intellectuality on the intellectual life of a nation; on its progress in literature, science and philosophy; on the production of men and women of genius—are bound to be unfavorable.

THE EDUCATION OF CHILDHOOD.

No one will pretend that a child is capable of studying philosophy as such, or of engaging in a philosophical or theological discussion in form and terms. But the child undoubtedly possesses the philosophical spirit. He wants to know both the what and the why. This spirit is much stronger in the average child than in the average adult who no longer cares about the why and wherefore of rainfall, being now only concerned in the fact of rainfall, its amount and its bearing on crops and prices.

What is true of physics as related to the curriculum of child life, is equally true of geometry. Geometrical figures are of a more vital, result-producing, percept-forming interest to children than they are to adults or to youth of the high-school period, wherein geometry is usually first presented as a subject of study. The high-school boy's interest in geometrical figures is incidental. It is required of him to study about them, and he does so because it is a part of the course and as a matter of personal pride in keeping up his marks and class standing. The interest of the child is deep, genuine, primitive, fundamental; and he is just as capable, during the years of the primary-school, of studying much of the facts—not the logical processes of formal demonstration—of geometry, as the high-school boy, with this difference in his favor, as before stated, that the study is of more real interest, his ideation more vivid, and its results, psychologically more permanent and more fruitful. His progress will be slower, of course, but surer. And in the primary-school the maxim should be, "Make haste slowly!" Haste, hustle, worry, with their attendant impatience and imperfect results, with their effects of "nervousness" on the part of teacher and taught, are out of place in the primary grades, particularly. Not that there should be dullness or dragging. Neither should there be rushing or driving. There should be the natural atmosphere of cheerfulness, of interest, and the natural movement and energy born of interest, not that haste born of the forcing process of commands, nagging and driving. The source of momentum in the primary-school should be from within, within the heart and mind of the child and with the united hearts and minds of teacher and child—not from without in the imperious will of teacher and principal.

The fundamental geometrical percepts formed in early life have a value increased in geometric ratio over the value of such percepts formed in high-school life, in that they come into play as formative ideas early, and are effective during the entire pre-high-school period—giving enlarged powers of perception and apperception, which influence helpfully all subsequent educational development.

A boy of six or seven learns readily such simple

geometrical percepts as straight line, curved line, broken line; angle, right angle, acute angle, obtuse angle; perpendicular line, oblique line, parallel lines; circle, diameter, chord, radius, circumference, arc, sphere, hemisphere. Later on he acquires the meaning of triangle, quadrilateral, polygon, square, rectangle, parallelogram; of cube, prism, pyramid, cone.

The drawing of these figures will be of great interest to the child. He can use the rule and pencil with interest and profit.

The boy of eight, or even of seven, can be led to see that a line perpendicular to one of several parallels is perpendicular to each of them. He will discover the fact, though no attempt should be made at a formal logical demonstration. He will discover that a diameter divides a circle into two equal parts; that a radius, perpendicular to a chord, bisects the chord and its arc; that every chord except a diameter divides the circle into two unequal parts; that an indefinite number of diameters may be drawn in the same circle; that all these diameters are equal, etc.

He can be taught in the second or third year of primary-school life to construct geometrical figures by geometrical rules, beginning with the construction of the circle. He can be introduced to measurement and simple drawings to scale. The importance of an early introduction to measurement, which plays so increasingly an important part in modern physical science and in all forms of industry and engineering, will be acknowledged. "As the twig is bent, so the tree is inclined." This old maxim applies to mental life as truly as to the bodily life and the character life.

Of course, this is no attempt to outline a detailed course in physics, geometry, or any other subject, for the guidance of instruction and training in the primary-grammar school, but rather to indicate the practicability of such an outline at the hands of expert educators, and to show that such courses as are here advocated are within the range of the development of the child and that such courses properly outlined and taught, will greatly facilitate that development, and will constitute the best possible, most economical and efficient, preparation for the taking up of advanced courses along the same lines. It is further contended that there will be both an increased development and a great saving of time, in that the child will be ready to undertake advanced courses at an earlier period, and at the same time be better prepared than now for the mastery of these courses.

And finally, it is pointed out that the range of subjects within the eight school years which constitute the entire life of most children—making the primary-grammar school the real school of the people

—will be extended so as to put in the possession of this majority of children knowledge and skill, which now they never attain. It would seem a wise, a patriotic thing, to focus educational attention upon these eight years of school life, and upon the possibilities of children during this period, remembering that whatever increases the range and efficiency of the educational experience and development of this important period will affect the entire system of higher education, acting and reacting positively and favorably upon all the schools—the colleges, the universities, the professional schools and the schools of engineering.

A nation depending, as this nation does,—for existence and progress in time of peace; for defence or aggressive attack in time of war (which often comes when least desired or expected)—upon the intelligence, initiative and patriotism of its people, whose sentiment is the source of government and law and the only bulwark for the maintenance of the one and the enforcement of the other—such a nation must give increasing attention to the education and training of its children. Such a nation must conceive of the education of its children as being its chief preoccupation and business. Educational questions in such a nation cannot have a merely professional, narrowed, pedagogic interest. They are of universal national import and are worthy the attention of the highest statesmanship and most exalted and most capable patriotism. In such a nation the teacher should stand in higher public and national regard than is now, as a rule, accorded in this country. In the future, a nation will be gauged by the esteem in which the teachers of its children are held. By this standard, the Germans already stand preëminent. In the achievement of German unity, and in the subsequent development of the Empire which embodies that unity, the "professor" has played an equal part with the soldier and is almost equally honored. The organic parenthood of the nation, as manifested in its educational sentiment and systems, should foster with peculiar care and power the manifold interests of its child-life.

This great republic, surpassing all nations in wealth and in the totality of its domestic and foreign commerce, with its amazing energy and fertility of material invention, is surely able to see to it that not one of its little ones should suffer from physical want or educational neglect. Its motto, in its provisions for its little ones, should ever be, "Get the best!" For the best is never a whit too good for the child—the best in school-buildings, equipment, and play-grounds; the best in courses of instruction, the best in the selection of instructors; and last but not least, the best in the way of physical nutrition and comfort. These tender offshoots of the nation's physical life should not be allowed— even one of them—to suffer as many of them do— pale and anaemic—from frost, cold and hunger, in want even of shelter and a comfortable sleeping-place, and of suitable clothing, in the fearful northern winter. In a nation which is one of the world's granaries and one of its great beef-markets, thousands of its own children go hungry to school and hungry to bed—while other thousands do not go to school at all and some—to the shame of the country —have not where to lay their heads.

To return to the subject of geometry-teaching in the primary-school: it can be said in brief, that the boy in the first four years of the primary-school can and should acquire the ability to construct a variety of geometrical figures. He can acquire intelligently the definition of these figures, thus attaining fundamental form-percepts, of value in all the after-study of mathematics. He can learn by degrees to analyze and to discuss these figures. For example, set a boy of nine, say, after the preliminary training of previous grades, to the examination of a right prism and does any one believe that this boy would fail to discover that the lateral edges of a prism are equal; the lateral faces, equal; that the faces are rectangles, etc. How much more this discovery will mean to the boy as a factor in his mental growth, as a stimulant to his mental development, than it would mean to have him, later on in the high-school, to commit the same facts to memory from a text-book. (Of course, actual models would be put before the child.)

Thus, what has been called "inventional" geometry, the facts of elementary geometry, their discovery by the child, geometrical definition and construction, and geometrical drawing, are fit subjects for primary instruction.

A significant fact, sought to be emphasized right here, is, that present subjects and methods under-estimate the mental force and range of child life in general and in particular the really tremendous potential nerve and mind energy of the American white boy—and though in somewhat lesser degree, by reason of the fact that his educational opportunities are frequently much less favorable, of the American colored boy. Children are put and kept at exercises and studies that do not interest them, because they fail to awaken the abilities of the children. They do not call out the child's energies. Hence arise indifference and dullness. Indifference occasions disorder and necessitates force or driving and even corporal chastisement. The child becomes a subject for discipline. He ceases to be a pupil, a learner, or disciple, and becomes a prisoner; and the teacher, a sort of jailer or policeman. The child mutinies and rebels; or he submits with a mental and emotional reservation that becomes an incentive to future outbreaks of disorder.

Referring again to the subject of physics, it is an appropriate subject for the primary grades, taught, not in its mathematical-philosophical aspect, but in its phenomenal or descriptive phases, by observation and simple experiments. The subject of electricity is one that has interesting and simple phenomenal phases that will appeal wonderfully to children when presented by the sympathetic, skillful instructor. Beginning with simple experiments in electrification, lessons can be graded and adapted leading on by slow, carefully-taken steps, to such other electrical and magnetic phenomena as are within the comprehension of children. Similarly, there could be performed with the assistance of the children under the teacher's direction, simple experiments in heat, light, sound, capillary attraction, etc. In short, a graded series of experiments can readily be devised by the skilled teacher who understands well the subject of physics, that would meet the child's interest in natural phenomena—an interest which is innate, and persistent, unless it is systematically repressed by unnatural methods on the part of teachers and parents. Children have a vast curiosity or active capacity of interest, which is too often misused because not educatively developed and directed. To command the entire range of the child's capacities of interest and action, and to control and develop them, is to go far toward a right education of him or her.

Present methods and systems in the way of manual and industrial training and of out-door playgrounds and out-door sports, are beginning to meet with some approach to adequacy the child's love for and need of physical action and exertion. But the child's capacity for knowledge is not met. He asks, in his very mental make-up and attitude, for bread, but he is given the husks of an a-b, ab; e-b, eb-system of education, which is in effect and fact a system of repression, of pedagogic "foot-binding."

The results of this neglect to make the course of study correspond with the child's curiosity or desire for knowledge, and with his capacity for the acquisition and assimilation of knowledge, are a waste of the child's capacity, a blunting of it, or a misdirection of it; secondly, a postponement to a later date of the study of things which the child ought already to have mastered, and which he must then acquire under the disadvantage of diminished emotional interest and motor response; thirdly, he must postpone still further or omit entirely, in the case of the majority of children, things he needs to know and master. Thus the principles of economy and efficiency are violated.

If an idea or percept is to be most potent or efficient psychologically, both in sheer persistence, and in power of assimilation through apperception, or of combination with other percepts to form larger units (concepts); or in capability to enter into the construction of ideals as products of imagination— then the given idea or percept must be acquired at the life-period of greatest cerebral plasticity or receptivity, of greatest emotional and motor response to perceptual stimuli.

Not that the given percept (any idea of reality gained directly through observation or experience) may not be acquired at a later period in apparently as short or even shorter time and with as much or even more apparent ease. But the given percept acquired later will not possess equal potential efficiency, psychologically speaking; will not possess an equal degree of what one might call affinity or power of attraction, assimilation or combination. The idea or percept itself as a sort of psychological atom or molecule will not possess the same inherent energy. For ideas or percepts (and percept-building is the chief business of the school for children), must be regarded as having powers analogous to the dynamic powers of the physical molecule, or the affinity powers of the chemical atom, or the attractive-repulsive powers of the hypothetical ion with its capacity of attracting or repelling electrons. There must be organic structure in the nerve-centers corresponding to every really distinct percept and as the physical concomitant of the mental processes of perception, recollection through association of ideas, of apperception or the differentiation of percepts, of imaging, of concept-forming, of judgment and reasoning, there must be analogous physical processes and an inter-play of nerve-force and nerve-currents analogous to electro-magnetic induction together with molecular, atomic and electronic changes accompanying and distinguishing every mental act and process, or every distinct class or grade, in the complex and hierarchy of such acts and processes. For we must necessarily conceive the mental life of which the brain and nerves—the cerebro-spinal system—are the body or organism, as being accompanied by a neural integration ordered by the same laws of nutrition and assimilation, growth, natural selection, and evolution within the neural organism, that we discover in the outer world of living forms.

Using an analogy from biology, it is interesting to consider a percept in its formation and development, through apperceptive assimilation, as comparable to a living protoplasmic cell, and as possessing and exercising analogous functions; and a concept, as a group of such percept-cells so correlated as to exercise a common psychologic function and to constitute a sort of psychologic tissue. The birth or generation of a percept would thus be analogous to the generation of a new life-cell. Indeed, it would seem probable that the generation and development of percepts and concepts are accompanied by the generation and development of neural cells and combinations of cells—tissue—as the material concomitants of mental development. Not that the relation of physical causation exists between these neural organs and processes and their mental correspondents or equivalents. For by no stretch of logic or imagination can, for example, the mental perception of a noise or a sound be represented as the result of the molecular vibrations which constitute noise or sound in the physical, objective sense. Vibrations can only produce vibrations. For while the conception of the transformableness of physical energy is philosophically acceptab'e, the transformation of physical energy into a mental equivalence—as consciousness, perception, conception, and the like—is incapable even of expression by any existing terminology.

Yet the capability and tendency of the human mind to assume states that correspond to the changes in environment, as registered in and by means of the brain, is a fundamental fact in psychology as related to the process of child education and training. For it is by the formal and orderly transformation or prearrangement of the environment, or of the stimuli that constitute it, that the teacher essays to induce changes in the mental complex and continuity of his pupils. And the more perfect his knowledge of the laws of the spontaneous powers of the mind; of the gradual, progressive ascent of this spontaneity to higher stages during the all-important period of adolescence, and of the reaction to stimuli of these phases in both their simultaneous and serial relationships—the more certain and sound the mental growth. Just how or why, except as the fiat of the Divine Creator, the soul or mind changes its modes, moods and attitudes, as self co-changes in rapport with other changes in the physico-psychic simultaneity—even as the cloud tints shift with the varying angle of the setting sun—is likely to remain forever inexplicable. But it is just these changes that reveal the world to the soul as the ever-present "co-efficient" or "function" of these changes, and the soul to itself as an entity or being alike conscious of changes in itself and perceptive of changes in that external complex and continuity of form and movement which we call environment.

In all study of the mind, and its development and education, curiosity and interest center about the brain and its connections. Even the materialist must pause in wonder, in astonishment, in presence of this marvellous gray-and-white substance—the ultima thule of physical refinement, delicacy, adap-

tiveness, and organization. Its extreme sensitive-
ness enabling the astronomer to perceive and study
the fragile light-waves from nebulae whose dis-
tances are incomprehensibly vast—its robustness
enabling the trained civilian to endure the extremes
of stress and strain incident to modern life—make
't the miracle of nature.

A more characteristic function of the brain than
that of mere telegraphic or telephonic or phono-
graphic functions, is its capacity, tendency and cer-
tainty to make itself a counterpart of the outer
world, an epitome or replica of both experience and
of environment as the external condition of experience. All soul or mind phenomena leave their
traces in the nerve tracts or ganglia; every nerve
node, once assumed in correspondence to either
impression or expression of the soul leaves its trace
and a tendency to reassume itself, to reappear. And
repetition of the stimulus but increases the tendency
to such reassumption or reapparition. All impressions from without and all expressions from within,
outward, register themselves in the brain, or rather,
they organize the brain in a dynamic or vital way.

And thus the brain, with its nerve-cells, nerve-centers, and nerve-fibers, and the reactions of nerve
energy among them, becomes more and more the
vicarious substitute for that environment with its
forms and forces. The impressions left in the brain

by the stimuli of environment and experience come to be studied instead of the stimuli. They become the neural equivalents of these stimuli. Thus is created an inner world of neural-mental equivalents, whose forms and forces, while in fact wholly different both in form and action from the world of external reality, yet present in consciousness an illusion of perfect similarity and almost of absolute identity. Problems are worked out and relations discovered which but for these mental-neural equivalents would be impossible of solution or discovery. And the business or aim of the schools, in this point of view, is to make the brain a correct replica of the environment so that its actions and reactions will bear at every stage immediate and complete correspondence or identity with reality as observed in nature and as experienced in correct bodily action, habits and conduct. In adult life, the mind is influenced only in an incidental way by the immediate direct influences of the physical environment. The adult mind lives in and through this inner world which is created during the period of adolescence, the building period—an inner world made up of neural-mental equivalents of experience-percepts; and their higher integration or differentiation-concepts.

Under right training the adolescent mind becomes the map or key to nature and history, and in the study of literature becomes "the heart of the world." Thus the brain becomes the complex finger-board on which the soul plays and by which it feels and hears the vibrations, the music, of man, earth, and the spheres; or the electric switch-board whose endlessly differentiated combinations unlock and direct the unmeasured stores of mental and physical energy—the energies alike of nature and of mind.

In no strained or irrelevant sense the universe itself becomes, thus, conscious, intelligent, vocal, in man, the man of ideal culture and character; in him "the heavens declare the glory of God and the firmament showeth His handiwork"; in him "day unto day uttereth speech; night unto night showeth knowledge."

The importance of so directing the education of childhood that the mind of the child shall, by means of first-hand impressions of reality, form a wide range of percepts—form them vividly so as to give them intense and permanent powers of growth and assimilation with a range wide enough to afford the sufficient basis for an after conceptual and ethical development which shall meet the varied needs and exigencies of an active and noble life—is readily granted. The percept is all-important. In its beginning, it occasions the rise of consciousness, and at the same time reveals the outer world through the variations in consciousness occasioned by the flux and rhythm of stimuli. Philosophy, Science and Education have their root in the percept—philosophy being based on the fact of consciousness to which the percept gives rise or occasion; science, based on the what or content of consciousness, being an orderly account and systematic arrangement of the differentiations of consciousness, as occasioned by changes in the stimuli of the environment, and resting on the assumption that there is a correspondence between the differentiations in consciousness and the differentiations in the environment, the intuition of which gives that sense of fact and reality which is the basis of scientific truth; education being concerned with the development of percepts and their organization into concepts as a means of so forming the intellect that it may become the efficient and reliable agent and servant of will and conscience—the ultimate goal of education and life itself being essentially and necessarily a moral one —the development of character.

The importance of the percept is recognized by Prof. William James who makes "percepts and concepts the two fundamental constituents of being and the function of thought proper the substitution of a conceptual order for the perceptual order in which experience originally comes, thought in its development creating a map of life which makes possible its revaluation." Thus it becomes the business of the primary-school or school of childhood to initiate and organize the perceptual order with such a wealth and energy of neural-mental equivalent-stimuli as to make it the fit material or nexus which "thought proper" shall transform into the conceptual order, which will and conscience in turn, by the alchemy—or algebra—of daily life, shall evaluate into the highest order—the ethical, or order of character.

The relation of physical health and bodily activity to mental health and activity is everywhere recognized, as well as the relation of the brain and nervous system to thought and mental growth. Bodily health, on which mental growth depends, becomes increasingly important when we consider that the brain, which depends on bodily vigor for its strength of action and development, has a double function—on the one hand it is the organ which controls and co-ordinates the physiological functions, and on the other hand it is the organ of mental-spiritual life and growth. And the brain, as the organ of mental life, must be an integration or higher organization of the brain as the organ of physiological regulation. And it is in connection with this higher integration—which is one, not of specifically differentiated organs in the brain, but rather of function, using existing nerve-paths and connections—lines and centers of nerve-force already developed in the exercise of physiological co-ordination—that the true mind-life manifests and functions.

Hence, no consideration is more practical or more fundamental, incidentally, in the pedagogy of childhood as related to the formation and development of a vigorous perceptual life as the basis for a higher conceptual and ethical life, than the health and vigor of the enveloping organism as body and brain. And this consideration becomes imperative in view of the fact, that the transformation and lifting of material from its condition when taken into the organism as food, to the highly refined condition of gray nerve-cells, presuppose and necessitate the expenditure of enormous energy even in the case of children who might grow up with no formal experiences of the schools. But the situation becomes a more serious one in the case of children in a civilized community where school life is a customary experience and where, hence, the nerve energy must be "forced", so to speak, in order to bring the nerve strength and tension of the individual children up to a degree commensurate with that of the life-stress of the adult group or community. Not only must the child's body furnish and transform the nourishment needed for the production of nerve force and substance, but this same body must lift itself from infancy to childhood, from childhood to adulthood, through the successive stages of adolescence. What a tremendous task is accomplished in this miracle of transformation and transition! It is an epitome of the ascent of life universal. Truly the child is literally maker of himself as an adult. What sympathy universal manhood should feel for the child —the coming man! And how is the heart of a father touched as he notes the growing indications of maturity in his son! A feeling of comradeship arises and, by and by, the son becomes the companion of the father. By nature's subtle, inexplicable ritual, divinely ordained, the son is initiated into the order and chapter of his father—the ancient order of man.

It will be acknowledged that a closer study, a deeper understanding, of the functions, hygiene, and development of brain and nerve cells in man and in child are needed to perfect systems and methods of education in face of the evident difficulties of the undertaking.

The study of science, that is, of natural phenomena, should commence with the beginning of the child's school life and continue till its close, in proper gradations as to method and content as related to the child's capacity. The same statement is pertinent as to the study of form and number (or quantity in both its spatial and numerical aspects including the graphic representation and measurement of quantities and their inter-relationships), that is, of mathematics, which is an indispensable instrument and agent of pure and applied science; of industry and engineering.

As a matter of course, it is assumed that the child, on entering school, should commence the study of numbers or arithmetic; and he should continue it without a text-book, in oral lessons, during the first four years, the teacher using blackboard, chart, objects, actual weights and measures and toy or school money, and the pupil using pencil and tablet. The instruction should be on the order of the older "intellectual" arithmetic, such as the well-known text of Warren Colburn. The four-years' course should cover the subjects of notation, numeration, the four fundamental numerical operations, simple factoring, the decimal system of United States money, the simple tables of weights and measures and their use in simple examples involving small numbers, and elementary percentage and elementary mensuration. The fifth and sixth years should be given to the mastery of a comprehensive text in modern physical and industrial arithmetic, while the seventh and eighth years should be devoted to the study of commercial or business arithmetic and to the practice of modern elementary double entry book-keeping, so taught as to afford incidentally a review of the principles and processes of arithmetic —together with a study of business forms and processes. Along the other mathematical line, after four years of the oral teaching of descriptive or phenomenal geometry, with much practice in geometrical-mechanical drawing, there should follow one year in elementary algebra with special attention to the simple equations of the first degree as a preparation for the formal study of logical geometry from a good text. Then should follow two years of instruction in plane and solid geometry in connection with a good text-book, and a final or eighth year in college or higher algebra, so taught as to constitute an introduction to analytic geometry.

As there are two lines of mathematical study which should be pursued simultaneously during the childhood school period—the eight-year primary-grammar or elementary period—so also there are two simultaneous lines of appropriate study in science—the physical or inorganic line and the biological or organic line. Along the inorganic or physical line, the order of studies would be as follows: Four years of oral lessons with simple experiments and illustrations in physics, chemistry, and mineralogy, to be followed by a fifth year's study of a good text in physical geography; a sixth, using a suitable text, in physics; a seventh, using a text, in elements of chemistry; and the eighth, using a text in mineralogy with qualitative chemical analysis. Free use would be made of apparatus, and there should be facilities for elementary laboratory work in physics and chemistry. Pupils would be encouraged to make much of the apparatus for experiments. Live, active boys twelve or thirteen years of age would take far more interest in this sort of study and experiment than the average college or high-school youth does at present, and would get far more out of it. And it is strange that educators have so far underestimated the ability of the intelligent, vigorous, American boy of from ten to fourteen years. Along the organic, vital, or biological line, of the curriculum in science, after four years of oral instruction in geography as nature-study, with special reference to agriculture and giving attention to the study of plants and animals and simple bacteriological phenomena—such as the fermentation of yeast, etc., which are intelligible to the average American boy of seven or eight—there would follow a text-book which would have to be written by some such competent authority as Prof. L. H. Bailey of Cornell, which would present geography in its biological aspect, with especial attention to soils, water, atmosphere, etc., as related to plants, animals, and especially to agriculture. This geography would treat of life—plant, animal and human—and the factors that support and condition life, and the occupations and industries which are connected with the artificial direction and propagation of living forms useful and necessary to man. After a year's study of such a geography, there would follow one year in elementary biology of plant and animal forms, one year in a text-book in agriculture and forestry proper, and one year, the last or eighth, using a text in human physiology and hygiene and sanitation. Attention would be given in each of these years to elementary bacteriology—as related to biology, agriculture and physiology.

Freehand drawing, together with coloring, is another line of educational practice appropriate to the elementary or primary-grammar school. This subject could well alternate or divide time in some ratio with mechanical drawing. Drawing is a subject of transcendent educational and practical value, and should occupy a place equal to that now held by arithmetic and reading. It is the language of mathematics, of mechanics, and of art in general. No subject makes a more universal, perennial or useful appeal to the interests and activities of the child. It is a useful adjunct to many other subjects. It affords a natural and helpful outlet for the energies of childhood. It should form a continuous part of the elementary curriculum. Its value is appreciated by both pupils and parents. Its relation as design to constructive industrial art in all its phases, makes it practically invaluable and indispensable, educationally.

Thus far no reference has been made in this discussion to handicraft or manual-industrial training or education. The educational, as well as vocational or practical value of manual-industrial training is now universally recognized. The child is to be trained not alone for thinking, but also for doing, if his training is to prepare for useful, well-rounded, and well-grounded living. Manual-industrial training appeals to the child's active and constructive powers, brings him into contact with reality, develops self-confidence and self-mastery, cultivates persistence and patience, strengthens will-power, and encourages neatness, order, system, and accuracy. The sense of touch, the physical judgment of distance and measurement, and the muscular sense, as well as muscular skill and control, are other valuable results of manual-industrial teaching and training, and this form of training should begin the first day of the child's school life and continue to its close.

As one of the useful materials for beginning this sort of training in the lowest primary grade, clay suggests itself—prepared clay. Its plasticity makes it available for the supple, unhardened hands of children. Then, children like to handle it and mould it into various shapes. Using models such as sphere, cube, pyramid, or natural objects, such as apple, orange, lemon, pear, a bunch of grapes, a saucer, a cup, etc., children can be trained to considerable enjoyable and valuable manual dexterity while attaining first-hand ideas of form in three dimensions. These clay products or articles can be colored in imitation of the natural originals, to the interest, delight and satisfaction of the children. The sand-board is successfully used to imitate relief-forms of land.

Cloth is another usable material at this stage, being pliable and easily handled. Using the needle and thread, boys in the four primary grades should be taught the elements of sewing as needlework. The educational value of needlework is that it requires close attention to detail, to "little things," the things of thread and stitches—a lesson of its own peculiar value. Then, too, it is not a bad thing for every boy or man, even, to be able to sew on a button properly, or to mend a rent in a garment, or even to patch and darn. Lessons in simple cooking are also entirely appropriate for boys in the primary-school grades. It is a strange but prevalent error, that men and boys do not need to know or learn cooking. Every intelligent person should know the principles of practical cooking—be able to cook rice, potatoes, or oatmeal; be able to make a stew or a hash; be able to make corn-bread or biscuit or light-rolls or bread, from yeast, flour, and other ingredients. So much depends in the way of human health, life and happiness on food, its preparation and economical purchase and use, that it presents itself as worthy of a place in universal primary education. Every educated man should be able to do good cooking along some branch of the art. Attention should be given to school-gardening, a subject whose importance is now fully recognized, especially in rural schools. Every human being should be a gardener, a florist—should learn to love flowers and plants and their cultivation.

In the fifth year of elementary school life—the first grammar-school year—wood is an appropriate material for manual-industrial training. The boy of ten or eleven years naturally desires a "tool-box", and now is the time for the school to turn this interest to the best account by giving him training in joinery, turning, wood-carving and cabinet-making. Two years can well be spent in wood-work or sloyd, one year in iron-work or forging, and one in the simpler principles of plumbing and fitting; of practical electrical construction; and in running simple engines of the steam and gasoline types. Of course, this plan would require shops for the boys at every grammar-school. And this is as it should be. Most boys leave school entirely at the end of the grammar-school period. Most of them will enter pursuits—industrial pursuits—calling for some mechanical knowledge and skill—and the grammar-school should furnish, not all the minutiae and details, but the elements or foundations of this knowledge and skill. The grammar-school would not be exactly a trade-school, but it would select from carpentry, blacksmithing, plumbing, and elementary electric and machine engineering, the fundamental, typical processes in case of each, and construct of these a practical educational synthesis for the training of the boys. Besides, the boy who learns the use of tools and the value of drawings in any one trade, can readily adapt himself to a different trade. In this respect he is unlike the adult mechanic who is an "old dog", to whom new tricks, even in his own trade, come hard.

All industrial work in the grammar-school period need not be comprised in a single course of study and practice. There might be electives. For example, the clay work recommended for the primary grades might continue as ceramics throughout the grammar-school, giving instruction and practice in pottery (lathe and kiln work), tile and brick-making, and concrete construction, now of such great and growing importance. Still other courses will suggest themselves.

Any one who thinks boys would not take to this sort of industrial practice, this interesting preparatory, "make-believe" work, knows nothing of boys, their likes and dispositions.

Another pertinent fact is this: such methods as

to science-teaching, and mathematics-teaching, and as to manual-industrial training, and as to training in book-keeping and business forms, in the grammar-school, would tend to keep the boys in the grammar-school; for many boys leave before they even complete the grammar-school grades. They leave because the instruction does not appeal to them, doesn't seem worth while. Also, as a corollary to this statement, the methods above suggested would be the means of many more boys entering the high-school and completing a course there—whereas now they are much in the minority in the high-school. It is a fact, that many boys who attend grammar and high-school, do so, mainly, because they are inclined to please their parents and not because they feel that they are getting "their money's worth."

No reference is made in this discussion, so far, to the teaching of reading, writing, spelling, grammar and composition, rhetoric and literature—in short to the subject of language in its various phases of thought expression. This subject, or these subjects, are already so much emphasized and so well distributed that they do not come within the range of this discussion, the purpose of which is to bring the phenomenal phases of science and mathematics down into the elementary grades, and to insist on the distribution and gradation of the subject-matter of the branches included, over the entire primary-grammar school period, as a means of securing fuller mental development, and of making the eight years of the school life of this period (which for most children will comprise their entire school life) more completely a preparation for an intelligent citizenship and for successful breadwinning or livelihood. And to insist, further, that drawing and manual-training are indispensable elements, also, for the elementary curriculum, and should form a continuous factor in it.

There are good grounds, however, for the statement that too much time is spent in language-study, including reading, writing, spelling, and grammar, or at least that the results are far from commensurate with the time and energy spent by teacher and pupil. It will also be granted that, notwithstanding the elaborate system of language-lessons and text-books, and illustrated, graded reading-books, together with intricate methods of teaching reading, designed to make progress rapid and easy, yet children taught by the old methods in vogue one or two generations ago, developed a stronger love for real literature, wrote a more correct, better composed or arranged letter, and had better knowledge of the meaning, spelling, use and derivation of words, than children trained under present methods. It is difficult for a child to make language, especially his own native tongue, an object

of study, because in childhood the mind finds difficulty in separating language from thought. Herein
we see a partial reason why there is greater culture
value in study of the classic or modern foreign language than in the study of English. Language
ought to be learned as far as possible in an incidental way; that is, incidentally to the accomplishment
of some other task. For example, a good way to
begin the teaching of reading to lowest or first grade
pupils would be to have a printed chart containing a
graded series of interesting gems of literature,
poetry and prose, to be memorized and studied, the
art of reading to be acquired incidentally to such
memorizing and study. Suppose the first of these to
be something like

> "Twinkle, twinkle little star!
> How I wonder what you are!
> Up above the world so high,
> Like a diamond in the sky!"

The object would be to memorize this little selection in connection with the printed lines on the
chart, to be able to read it orally, and to point out
the correct sight-symbol of the spoken word on the
chart, in proper sequence and with proper emphasis
on words and parts of words, the words of two syllables having the syllables divided with a heavy dash
on the chart.

There should be no haste in the memorizing and

correlating of sight-symbols with sound-symbols—printed words with spoken words—in connection with the first memory gem selected for instruction. The one given is not necessarily the best one. A simpler one could be selected. But the first one and all that followed, whether poetry or prose, should be selected from actual classic literature, within the comprehension of the children. And what has been said of science and mathematics is also true of literature: that is, real literature has its simple phases or selections that can be used in the primary-school, and nothing but selections from the best literature, literature worth knowing, studying and memorizing, should have any place in the schools or in any grade of the schools. Made-up school literature is of doubtful, or, at best, of ephemeral value. If a taste for real literature, the literature of the Bible and of the standard authors is to be cultivated, then only real literature should have a place in the school curriculum.

Returning to the first-chosen selection, there should be no haste in studying it. In its mastery by the method above suggested, several valuable results would be attained: the child would learn that spoken words have a graphic or sight equivalence, and vice-versa, that certain sight or written symbols have an oral equivalence; second, that the order of the sight symbols and their emphasis corresponds to the order and emphasis of the spoken words. Not that the child would know these facts as a formula or general statement, but he would know in a practical, concrete, or perceptive way.

The next step, after learning the selection as above indicated, would be to have each child typewrite the selection, using a machine whose keyboard would have letters similar to the chart letters, the teacher instructing the little ones how to use the machine. There should be one or two writing-machines in every grade of every school. Perhaps a simplified form of a practical typewriter will yet be brought down in price so that each pupil could have his own individual machine. Educators have been slow to recognize the educational value of the typewriter in the public school. It is destined to general use in schools in connection with the teaching of correct word-forms or spelling, and in composition exercises, particularly letter-writing and business forms.

The first-grade boy, in transcribing his first lesson in reading on a writing-machine, will learn that the sight-forms or printed words are made of parts—letters—in a certain order or sequence for each particular word. No effort should be made by the teacher at this stage to teach the names or values phonically, of the letters. As for the names of the letters, the pupils' own curiosity and interest in finding letters on the key-board to correspond with the letters of the selection or quotation on the chart, will awaken in him a desire to know the names, at least, of the letters, and even if he is not taught them formally at all by the teacher, he would find them out from older pupils or from his parents at home. The children would be allowed to keep their type-written lesson on slips of paper to be taken home for exhibition and discussion in the home circle.

This method of memorizing selections from literature in connection with the printed form of the selections should be continued during the first, second and third years of the primary-school on graded, printed, reading charts. Results valuable in two important directions would be secured: First, the child would be learning to read in a natural, rational way, incidental to the memorizing of the selections; second, he would be storing his memory with valuable literary material which would serve as a nucleus for the study of literature from text-classics in subsequent grades.

Reading taught and learned in this way would prove to be an interesting, intellectual and emotional stimulus. Attention could be paid to expression in elocution, and the child unencumbered with the minutiae of learning letters, syllables, sound and diacritical markings, would grasp the words, sentences, and meaning as a whole, and be free to give proper expression to the sight-forms. Nothing is more educative to the child than intelligent oral expression under the stimulus of interest and emotions awakened by the thought and sentiment of literary sight-forms, and their proper oral expression or elocution. The child would learn to read as he learns to talk—in sentences, and under the influence of an interest that would have an objective excitant, and an adequate or sufficient motive—the motive being the memorizing of the selections, or rather, the sense of mastery, and of emotional and intellectual pleasure, attendant upon memorizing; and the stimulus (or stimuli rather) being the printed sight-form as an object of curiosity and interest, and the teacher's oral interpretation of the sight-form.

Then, too, the practice of type-writing the selections, which should be kept up during the three years, would be of great value in clinching correct word-forms in the child's sight-memory, while, since the child by the law of association constantly associates and recalls the sound equivalents as he reproduces the sight-forms—ear- or sound-memory would also be developed by one of the most remarkable powers of the human brain, namely, that of transforming the potential ideation gained from one sense-organ directly to sensor equivalents in the brain tract devoted to the ideation of a different sense-organ. Furthermore, as a matter of fact, in three years of such a teaching of reading as this, in which the teacher would resolutely avoid any reference to the names of letters or spelling, seeking only to familiarize the child with correct oral expression of the printed forms, the child would learn the letters, and much of the sound values of letters, and syllables in spelling, without any aid whatever from the teacher. Thus a vast amount of "grind" now used in teaching letters and syllables would be avoided.

At the beginning of the fourth year, spelling would be taken up formally, using a good text-book in which the words would be arranged by their phonetic classification and resemblances. And of such books the writer regards the old "Blue-Back" or Webster's Speller as the best, judged by the comparative results of its use.

Spelling, as now taken up at the beginning of the fourth year, should be designed and taught strictly with the idea of giving the child skill in the powers or phonic values of letters in combinations, in a purely mechanical-phonic way, so as to enable the child to pronounce correctly any regularly-spelled word in the language, and to pronounce and spell the ordinary words which present phonetic irregularities. There should be a constant use of the typewriter in the spelling class. The aim should be to prepare the child to take up reading from a well-edited reading-book, containing only selections from standard literature which are within the range of his intellectual development, with illustrations which should be reproductions of master-artists in engraving and painting. It will be noticed that reading as suggested above is the reverse in process, from reading he would now be taught to do from his reading-book. By the method above suggested for teaching beginners to read, he would be transferring or translating the significance of ear or sound symbols to sight or printed symbols. After he has learned how to do this, so that the eye or sight-symbols come to stand directly for ideas, he is then prepared for the reverse process, of transferring eye or sight-symbols of his reading-book into the sound or oral symbols of elocution or good reading. This fourth year, spent in formal spelling, would thus be an intermediary year, designed to give the child a mechanical or phonetic skill in the powers of letters in combination—a mechanical facility in pronunciation.

A word here as to selections made for children's readers. There is a predominant idea that in making selections for readers for children, novelty should be the criterion, and selections are ruled out because they were included in the reading-books of a former generation. In this way, productions of classic excellence, are made to give way to new pieces of no standing in literature. Because certain recitations were included in reading-books used by the father or grandfather of the child, is a poor reason for excluding them from the books of the children of the present generations. Any one who will compare some of the reading-books of the hour with the old books for children, will be struck with the inferiority of the former. The old recitations are ridiculed, when the truth is, such a one as "Bingen on the Rhine," for example, is of perennial interest and beauty. Even "The Boy Stood on the Burning Deck," is better than many of the ephemeral, mediocre selections, and "made-up" school literature of the period.

It will be objected, that what is here outlined as appropriate and necessary in the education of the child, will overcrowd the curriculum, and add to the burdens of the already overburdened school-boy. But it will be appropriate to answer that most of the instruction in the four primary years would be oral, and the child's activities would be oral, observational, manual, and experimental, while the variety of instruction and activities would appeal to the variety of the boys' interests. Life is complex and so is human nature—and child nature and the curriculum should correspond to the range of the interests and activities of childhood. At present the burden of educational methods in vogue rests on the optic nerve, which is overtaxed by the constant perusal of text-books. The burden must be distributed to the auditory and tactual nerves, and the vocal chords and muscles, especially those of the hand and arm. A school day affords time for six half-hour, or nine third-hour, periods, before noon, and four half-hour, or six third-hour, periods, after noon. Within this time the work here suggested can be organized efficiently and carried forward by live, prepared teachers.

The departmental system now confined to high-schools could well be introduced as to certain subjects in the primary-schools and doubtless will be introduced. The class-room teacher would teach, say, such subjects as reading, numbers, geometry and geography, while special department teachers would instruct successive classes in such subjects as drawing, mechanical and freehand; manual-industrial art; physical science; biology; and music and physical culture—with separate departmental rooms and instructors for each of the subjects named. This departmental method would relieve the regular grade or class teacher, and give variety and movement and added interest to the children's work.

In some such way as here suggested it is entirely possible to construct and organize a curriculum and daily schedule which will meet and satisfy the whole range of the activities and interests of childhood.

The great subjects through which the mind realizes and organizes itself into individuality (perceptual being), personality (conceptual being), and character (ethical being), are broadly: the Sciences, in their dual aspect as mechanical or physical on the one hand, and as vital, biological, or organic on the other; Mathematics, as geometry, and as number or arithmetic; Manual-industrial art; Drawing, Mechanical and Freehand; Singing and Physical Culture; Reading, Composition and Elocution.

Along these lines of knowledge and action, which are themselves the priceless results of the body, mind, and heart struggles and developments of the centuries and the ages, the curriculum and schedule of the school for childhood—the primary-grammar school of the eight-year school period of childhood—should be organized to provide instruction, and action or practice, as the means of mental-moral unfolding and growth.

Nothing has been said of conduct or moral training. Yet every act of mind or body is a moral act —either good or bad—and every act has a moral quality which is its distinguishing underlying characteristic—its very essence or heart. Every mental act is mental-moral and has its moral sign or coefficient. Just as electricity is necessarily either positive or negative, so all human activity is either morally good or morally bad. No act either of body or mind is neutral; even involuntary, reflex, or instinctive action in man—in human nature—has a moral quality determined by the prevailing or dominant voluntary moral motive, will, choice and disposition. Just as every particle of matter has weight in addition to all its other properties, so every act has a character, a moral drift or tendency. Morality is the true organizing, conserving force in life and education. It is the governor of the engine of human activity. And the underlying motive of the education of children must be the attainment of character as expressed in such phrasal terms as purity, industry, honesty, kindness, honor, truthfulness and the like. And the whole drift of school organization and action should be toward character development. It is the touchstone, the supreme test, the final goal. And all systems and methods are most efficient when they are so organized and conducted that while meeting lesser or lower ends they also contribute positively to this highest end.

The whole structure of the ocean-liner—its hull, its machinery, its crew—is intended to enable it to carry its cargo into port. In this connection the school system is the ship; the teachers are the crew; the superintendent is the captain at the helm; the children are the precious cargo—and the port is character.

Hence, the very atmosphere of the school—its unconscious organic influence as well as its consciously ordered plans, purposes, and activities, must conduce to character-building in child nature. The physical cleanliness and neatness of buildings, appurtenances and premises; the orderly, prompt movement of its scheduled exercises; the direct personal influence of the teachers; the group tone and spirit of its pupils in class-room and on playgrounds—all these are factors in an organic influence that should be stimulative, directive, and formative of character in the children.

Nor in emphasizing the need of a broader, deeper intellectual development for children is it meant to minimize physical development and culture. The increased interest in such development and culture is one of the hopeful "signs of the time." Play, fair, earnest play, games and sports are among the indispensable factors in the development of the child.

As to the relation of the Bible to the public schools, it is one of the anomalies of a civilization founded on the Bible, on freedom of its interpretation and of religious worship and opinion, that the Bible, which has been so potent an inspiration in creating and shaping this civilization, should be excluded from the public schools. And stranger still that it should be an Old World element of recent assimilation that leads in the demand for such exclusion, coming as this element does from lands where they have suffered limitation and persecution because of the absence of religious and political freedom which this Book has secured. The very Book they oppose is the Book whose influence has formed the principles of human freedom and democracy which make possible their presence and citizenship in America—yea, that gives the very freedom they use in demanding its exclusion from the schools of the American people. This is a Christian land and the open Bible in every schoolroom should be the symbol of its Christian civilization.

If it is lawful to put Bibles in hotels and cars—and no one has denied this—it is lawful to put the Bible into the schools. Yea, and to have it read—without sectarian comment. The spirit of Continental rationalism is un-American and should not be permitted to exclude the Bible from the public schools. This spirit has atrophied the spiritual life of *France* with its declining birth-rate and diminishing population. It threatens Germany, the birthplace of religious freedom, where the Bible was first translated into the vernacular. And it dares to close in the schools of American children that Book whose spirit and teachings underlie Anglo-Saxon civilization, law, government and literature—that Book which symbolizes at once freedom and order; progress and conservation; work and worship; faith and knowledge.

The free and open Bible in that matchless version of King James which makes it the very paragon of English literature (a version so pure and perfect as to lead one to believe the translators were under divine guidance and inspiration) is the peculiar and priceless treasure and inspiration of the Anglo-Saxon race—a people combining the qualities of the Teutonic chivalry with the religious capacities of the Hebrew—a people whose westward trend, whether blazed through continental forest or pushing over lakes, streams and mountains; over deserts and glaciers; or over seas—has been the track of empire. Who doubts but that its abandonment of the Bible would mark the beginning of its decline?

The Bible, or at least selections from it, such as the Twenty-third Psalm, the *First* Chapter of Genesis, the Sermon on the Mount, the Nineteenth Psalm, the Thirteenth Chapter of the First Corinthians, the Sixth Chapter of the Ephesians, should be memorized and often repeated—including also the Ten Commandments and the Lord's Prayer. It is the lack of the restraining influences of that moral-religious truth most efficiently set forth in Scripture that accounts in large measure for the unsatisfactory results of popular education. Religion in some form is inseparable from human nature. No group of people, that is no race or nation, has ever risen to power apart from a religion, and it declines when its religion loses its force and sanction. Religion has been the unifying, directing force, in the development of nations and in the persistence of race-types. It is fundamental as to all other institutions of civilization and profoundly influences even the family life which necessarily is the most elementary of human institutions. The Hebrew is the most persistent of Aryan race-types, and the Hebrew has clung most unchangeably to the religion of his race.

The American public school should be characterized by a sanely religious, unsectarian spirit. It should be distinctively Christian, for only thus can the public schools accomplish their high mission in a Christian nation. This does not mean that there should be any churchism or ecclesiasticism, for Christianity is broader than any church. It is the religion of democracy which is its product; for there was never a true democracy apart from Christianity. In the teachings of Paul lie the germs of all modern liberty and energy of progress; for the spirit of Christ has been the key that has unlocked all the bondages of men whether these bondages were religious, intellectual, moral, political, or physical.

THE EDUCATION OF CHILDHOOD.

Intellectually, the business of the schools for childhood is the development of strong vital percepts or ideas by means of the fundamental human arts and sciences preparatory to the acquisition of concepts or general notions in scientific form and their use and organization as instrumentalities to useful and efficient thinking and living. And the fundamental human arts and sciences must have their roots in the primary school.

The fundamental percepts or ideas which the primary-school should develop correspond to the "mother ideas" of Pestalozzi, and they should be acquired as he insisted they should be: that is, not in a second-hand way through books, but first-hand, by the observation and handling of things themselves. "The relation of percepts to concepts," says Prof. William James, "is that of sight to touch."

Pupils developed along the lines herein suggested would be superior in every educational way to pupils who are trained, but at the same time suppressed, by present methods. The high-schools everywhere, by virtue of better prepared entrants, would be more truly and completely what they have been called, namely, "the colleges of the people." While colleges and universities and professional schools would become conscious of the impulse and uplift due to the general trend of an intellectual awakening among the youth of the nation. The improvement sought for in the colleges and universities must come from below. The standard of the primary-grammar school must be raised. The child is really imprisoned by present methods. He waits the liberation at your hands. "Loose him and let him go!"

There is too much intellectual barrenness in the child's curriculum. It is sometimes a desert rather than a child-garden. An American writer (Mr. McCready Sykes) has recently remarked: "It has been said that as each century has in a way its own distinguishing characteristics, the twentieth century has started out as the Century of the Child. * * * We are coming to realize the profound significance of the prolonged infancy of man. Alone among created beings, man attains maturity only after a long span of years. As civilization advances, the meaning of that long stretch of formative life comes into clearer and clearer view. And as for the children themselves * * * (with) their serene and trustful outlook on the world about them * * * they are more than ever dwellers in the *Interpreter's* House, nearer perhaps than the rest of us to the councils of the gods."

Truly, the child as yet is neither understood nor trusted. He is underestimated, undervalued. Yet, he is in truth, "the father of the man." Helpless and ignorant, though at the same time he is intelligence incarnate, the child faces the unknown in his weakness, and smiles, because he has faith; because he is faith itself. No wonder the Great Teacher took a little child and set him in the midst of them and said: "Except ye become as this little child, ye shall not enter into the kingdom of heaven." It is a striking thing that all the heathen religio-philosophical systems seem to have missed the significance and mission of childhood and to have disregarded, distrusted, or even disliked the child, some even to the extent of the sacrifice of children to placate infernal deities. But Christianity, creator of free science, free education and free religion, makes the child its symbol and the welfare and education of the child its highest mission.

The child of the future will be a splendid creature, and through him will arise a splendid humanity and civilization. Man must be lifted up by the lifting up of the child. The surest way to exalt manhood is to purify, strengthen, exalt and protect childhood. By all and every means at its command Christian civilization must protect the child from those corrupting influences and institutions which still mar the purity and strength of that civilization, and especially from the anti-Christian, anti-educative, morally, mentally, and physically disintegrating influences of the drink habit and traffic. For strong drink is an antidote to the educational process, tending, as it does, to the atrophy, coagulation, and paralysis of the delicate neural processes of the cerebrum, on which education and the higher life of man—the life intellectual, moral, and spiritual—depend.

Meanwhile let the teacher be the voice of one crying in a wilderness of educational confusion and misconception: "Prepare ye the way for the child! Make straight his path!"

THE ORIENTAL AND THE OCCIDENTAL WRITTEN LANGUAGES.

True education and true science are corollaries or complements, mutually. The wonderful East, despite its progress in some directions and its power in others, despite the antiquity of its culture, missed both. One reason for this, or at least one factor in the complex of reasons, may be the differences in the development of the written languages of the East and West respectively. The languages of the West, beginning with the Greek and its kindred the Latin and coming on to and including the chief modern languages of Europe and America are phonetic essentially; that is, in these written languages the letters and syllables have an immediate phonic value or equivalence, thus making the written or sight language the immediate replica, the intimate responsive environment, the sensitive differential, of the oral language, and thus of thought itself.

Such languages, thought and language reacting directly each on the other, become the powerful and accurate instruments of thought and bear a close relationship to reality. They become the languages of fact and reality, and thus are adapted to the development of truth—philosophic, historical, and scientific truth—as based on fact and reality. The phonetically-correlated written or sight language, while stimulating thought, at the same time controls it, or is capable of such control, thus preventing or discouraging unbridled extravagances of the imagination and keeping the foot of thought ever on or near the solid ground of reality and fact —that is, of truth. For language is a device for the expression and preservation of truth, and certain languages seem better adapted to this end than certain others.

The Oriental languages are essentially ideogrammatic or hieroglyphic, and not phonetic. In them there is no phonetic relationship between the written language—the written alphabet and syllable— and the oral speech. This accounts for the complexity of the Oriental languages, the difficulty the Western mind encounters in mastering them, owing to the vast number of different ideographic symbols necessary to express different objects and actions; to the fact that the oral names of these characters bear no phonic relationship to the characters themselves. In short, the Oriental word-signs are not sound-symbols. The superiority of the Western phonetic languages in which approximately no more elementary word-signs or letters are needed than there are vocal elements in the spoken tongue is apparent. In short, the Oriental written languages have no true alphabet in the Western sense—that is, no set of graphic symbols corresponding approximately in number and meaning or use, to the oral symbols of the spoken language. Hence, to master an Oriental written language or literature, a vast number of arbitrary word-signs, or historically-modified hieroglyphs, must be arbitrarily learned by committing their forms to eye or sight memory, the oral equivalent to each written word-sign affording no key to the written word-sign as a whole or as to the graphic elements which compose it. Thus the Oriental written languages are lacking in that direct phonetic relationship to oral speech, and through it, to thought itself, which is necessary for a mutual control and check or balance between the written and spoken tongues, and between the development of thought and the development of thought-expression in literary, philosophic or historical literature.

Hence it follows that the Oriental literature fails to maintain the proper balance between fact and reality on the one hand, and imagination or speculation on the other. Hence, too, there is no reliable history recorded in Oriental tongues; there has been no development of science. Its literature has been the literature of an extravagant mystic philosophy and poetry which bear little relation to fact, reality, or truth. There has been culture but no true development of rational education which is based on fact and truth, which in turn make possible scientific conceptions and principles.

On the other hand, the Western or Aryan mind, by the superior force of a more robust, decisive, inventive, aggressive personality and heredity, bridged the chasm between objective and subjective language, or rather, between language by sight and language by sound; between the graphic mark or symbol for objects and actions in the external environment, and the spoken word or sound-symbol—by giving the external graphic symbol a phonetic value —by establishing between the external graphic or sight-symbol and the spoken word or sound-symbol, standing for the same object or action, an immediate and continuous phonic correspondence and equivalence. Let *A* represent a graphic sign or mark used as the sign of any object or action in environment or experience, and suggesting by sight the idea to the mind of the given object or action.

Let *B* represent the spoken word or sound-symbol which suggests by sound the same idea to the mind of the given object or action.

Let C represent the common idea suggested through sight by A and through sound by B.

Then we have the following formulas as applicable to the Oriental languages:

C corresponds to or varies as A.

C corresponds to or varies as B.

But A does not correspond to or vary as B.

And B does not correspond to or vary as A.

In the case of the Western or Aryan languages:

C corresponds to or varies as A.

C corresponds to or varies as B.

And A corresponds to and varies as B.

And B corresponds to and varies as A.

That is, in the case of the Western or Aryan languages, A and B are mutually variable or mutually correspondent. In other words, in the Western or Aryan language scheme or system, the sight and sound languages—that is the written and spoken languages—are mutually correspondent and mutually variant. Or perhaps we might more strictly say, to borrow a mathematical phrase, that the sight languages of the Aryan people are a function of their sound languages, thus making them approximately the perfect written tongues. While in the case of the Oriental languages, the sight language or written language is not in general a function, variant or correspondent of the spoken tongue. This difference in language must be the index of a deeper difference in mental functioning and perhaps explains, in part at least, the "mystery" of the East and the difficulty felt by the Western mind in fathoming the mind Oriental. Thus, racial differences are not superficial, but lie deeper in the mental, social, political and religious, as well as physical or ethnological heredity of the races. And language is one of the most important indices, as well as instruments, and stimuli, of human development. The Greek tongue, the most perfect of the historic phonetic languages, must thus have been both a result and an efficient cause in Attic development, and its study must always remain a valuable means to mental culture and development, and a key to the development and achievements of that marvelous and brilliant people whose development and achievements helped in no strained or irrelevant sense to make modern science possible. And it was their wonderful language which made possible and stimulated their development and achievements.